Human Body
A to Z

SMITHSONIAN INSTITUTION

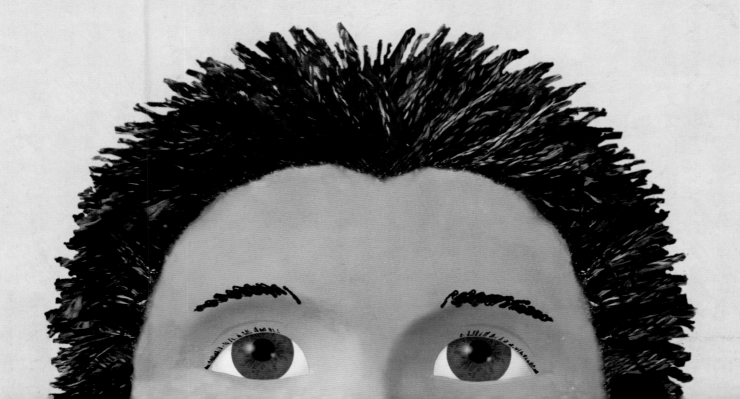

For Liz Greene Dufresne, my mentor, teacher, and most of all, friend.—LGG

To the kids of Chiaravalle Montessori and EKF Martial Arts. Thanks for the inspiration!—JM

Book and audio © 2012 Palm Publishing
and the Smithsonian Institution, Washington, DC 20560.

Lyrics, musical arrangement, performance and audio production by Mark Humble

Published by Soundprints, an imprint of Palm Publishing, Norwalk, Connecticut.
www.soundprints.com

Editor: Jamie McCune
Book design: Lindsay Broderick

First Edition 2012
10 9 8 7 6 5 4 3 2 1
Manufactured in China

Acknowledgments:

Carol LeBlanc, *Vice President*, Smithsonian Enterprises
Brigid Ferraro, *Director of Licensing*, Smithsonian Enterprises

    Our very special thanks to Don E. Wilson, for his curatorial review of this title.
    Soundprints would also like to thank Ellen Nanney and Kealy Wilson at Smithsonian Licensing
for their assistance in the creation of this book.

BONUS!

To **download** your MP3 files, e-book and printable
activities included **FREE** with your purchase of this book:

1) Go to **www.soundprints.com**
2) Click on "BONUS MATERIALS" at the top of the home page
3) Follow the easy directions!

Library of Congress Cataloging-in-Publication Data

Galvin, Laura Gates, 1963-
  Human body A to Z / by Laura Gates Galvin ; illustrated by Judy MacDonald. -- 1st ed.
    p. cm. -- (A to Z)
  ISBN 978-1-60727-296-0 (pbk.)
  1. Human physiology--Juvenile literature. 2. Human body--Juvenile literature. I. MacDonald, Judy, 1963- ill. II. Title.
  QP37.G35 2011
  612--dc23
               2011027520

Human Body

A to Z

by Laura Gates Galvin

Illustrated by Judy MacDonald

Soundprints™

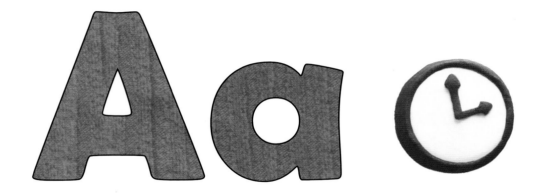

A is for Anatomy

Scientists study anatomy
to learn all there is to know
about the human body
from your head down to your toe!

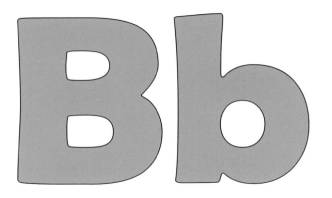

B is for Brain

Your brain is what's in charge of almost everything you do, like thinking and remembering and moving your body, too.

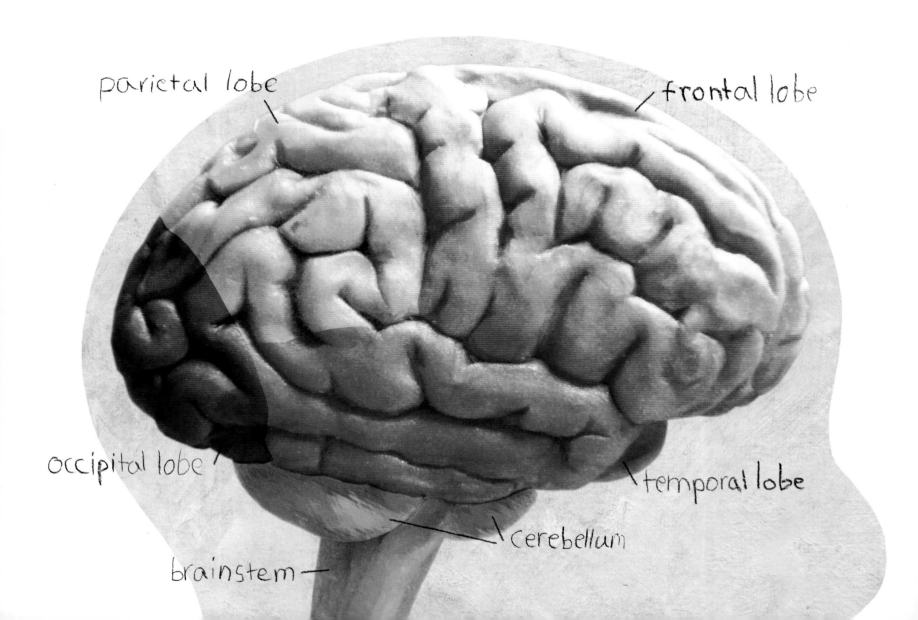

parietal lobe

frontal lobe

occipital lobe

temporal lobe

cerebellum

brainstem

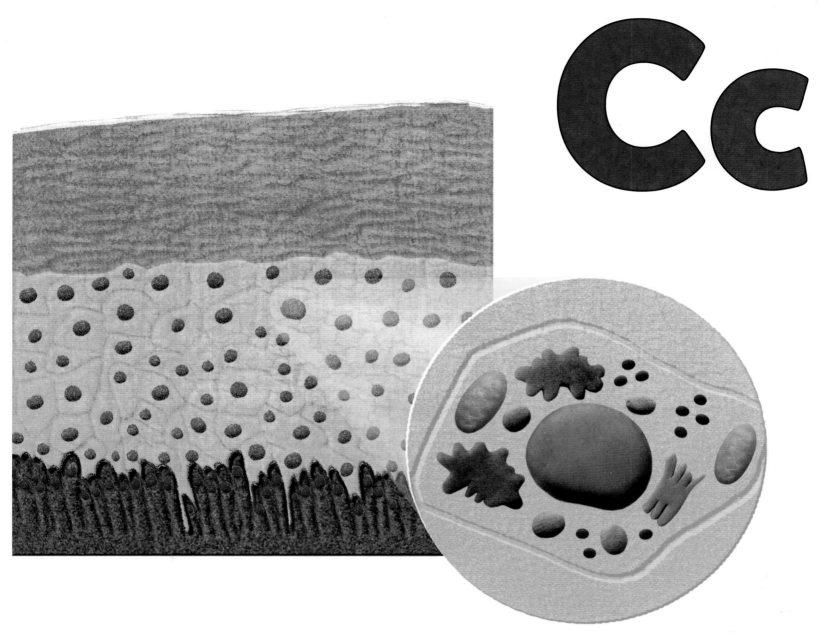

C is for **Cells**

Bodies are made up of cells,
trillions of them in all!
Picture them like building blocks,
or bricks that form a wall.

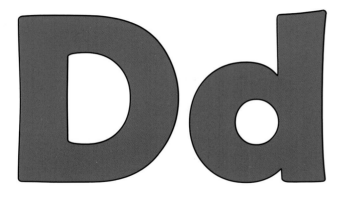

D is for **Digestive System**

Digestive organs break down food with the help of muscles in a group. The nutrients are then absorbed and the leftovers become poop!

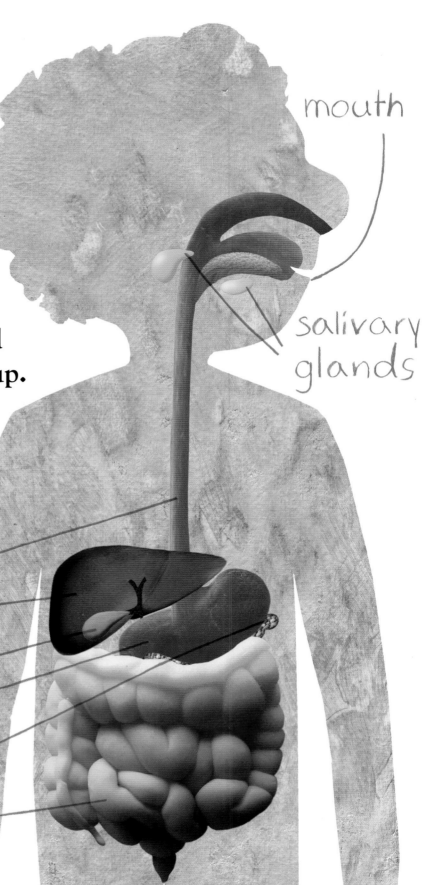

mouth

salivary glands

esophagus

liver

gall bladder

stomach

pancreas

intestines

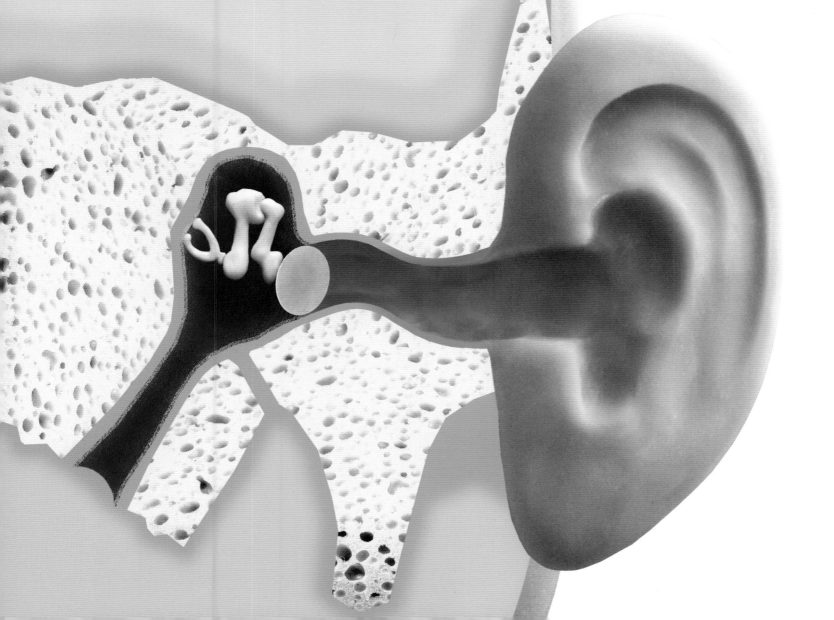

E is for **Ear**

Your ears have an important job,
with them you hear, it's true.
But did you know your inner ear
helps you to balance, too?

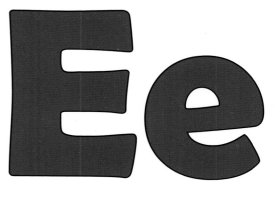

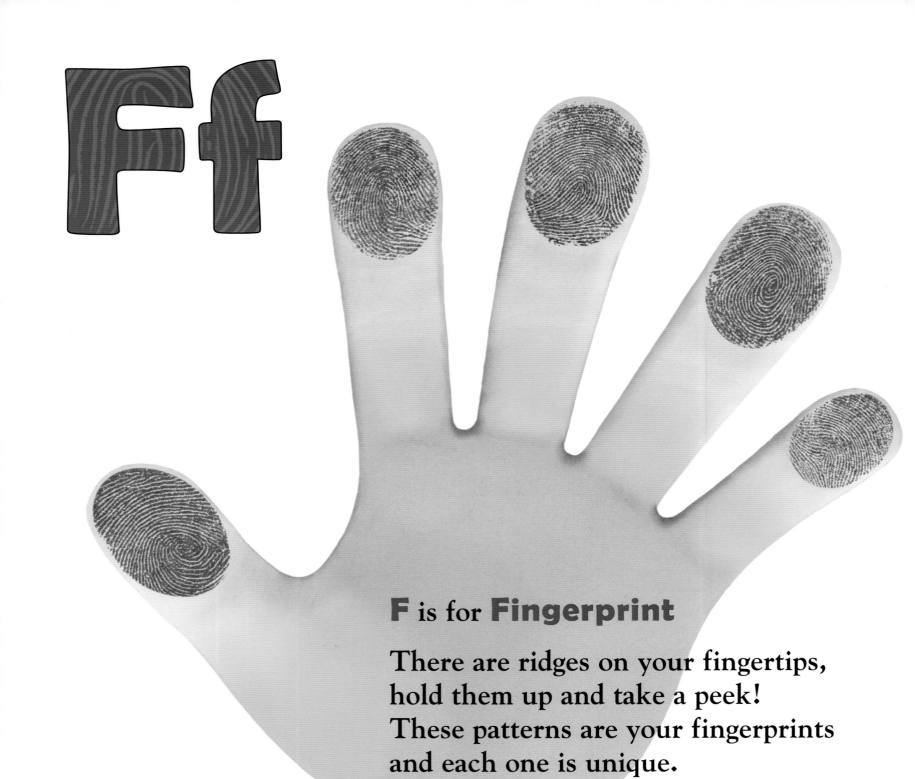

F is for Fingerprint

There are ridges on your fingertips,
hold them up and take a peek!
These patterns are your fingerprints
and each one is unique.

G is for **Gluteus Maximus**

This is your biggest muscle,
used to climb and jump or bow.
It's called the *gluteus maximus*.
You might be sitting on it now!

Hh

H is for Heart

Your heart is found inside your chest.
It pumps to make blood flow.
When you exercise, your heart beats fast
but when you sleep, the beat is slow.

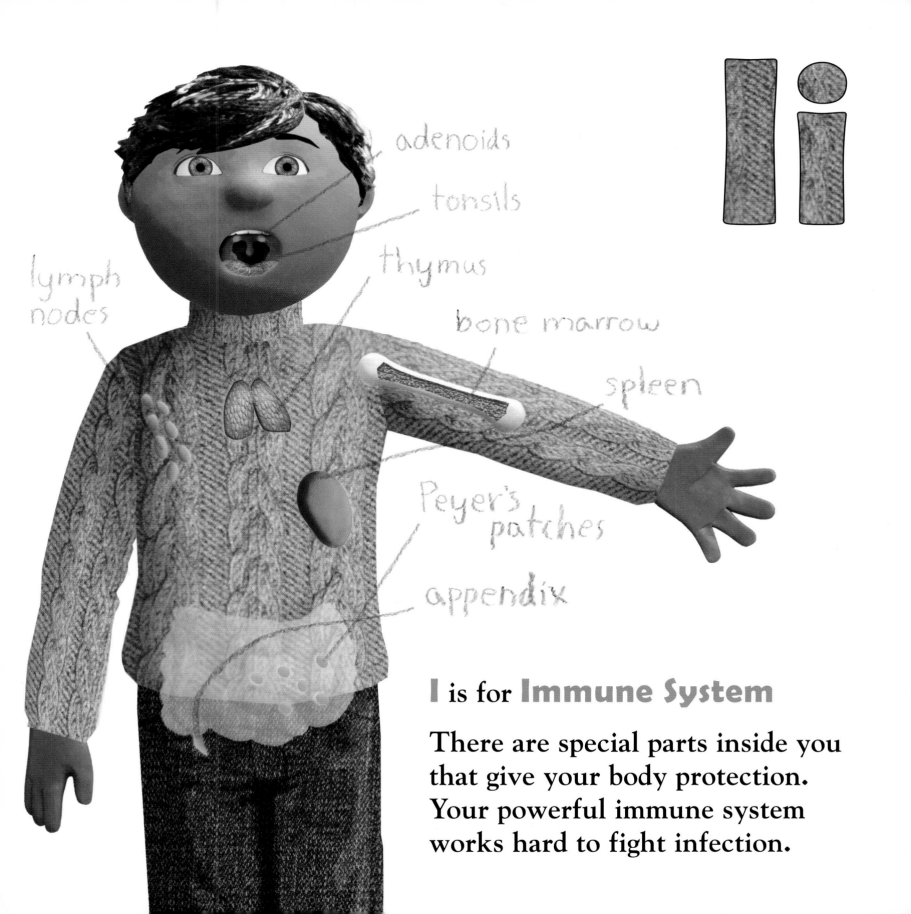

adenoids

tonsils

thymus

bone marrow

spleen

lymph nodes

Peyer's patches

appendix

I is for **Immune System**

There are special parts inside you that give your body protection. Your powerful immune system works hard to fight infection.

J is for **Joints**

Most bones meet at a hinging joint,
like your elbow or your hip.
They help you perform special moves,
like a karate chop or flip.

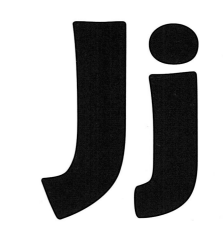

Kk

K is for **Keratin**

You have a protective layer on your hair, nails and skin. It's a certain type of protein, and it's called keratin.

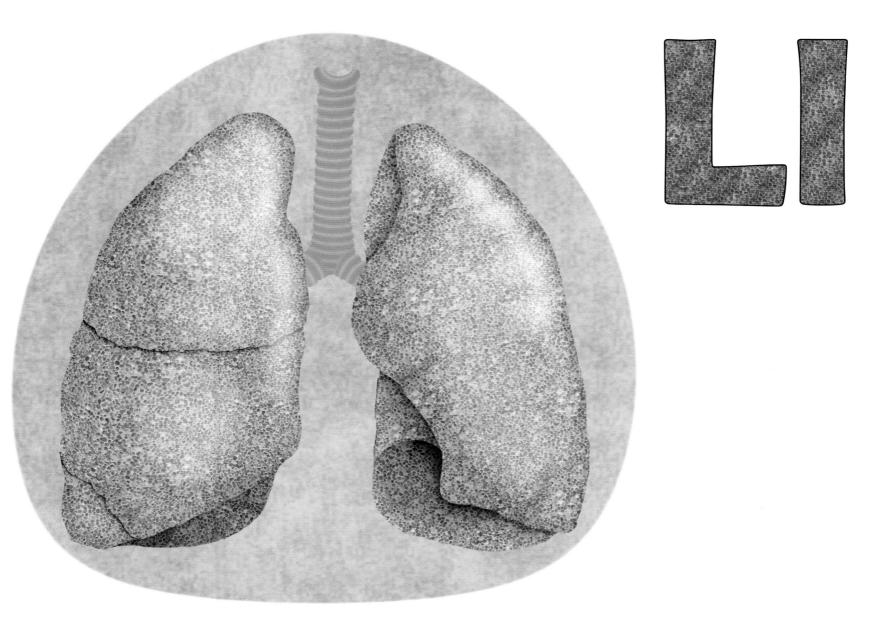

L is for **Lungs**

What happens to the air you breathe?
It flows through your mouth and nose.
It travels down your windpipe,
and to your lungs it goes!

Mm

M is for Muscles

Each person has many muscles—
over 600, that's a fact!
They help to make our bodies move
as they relax and then contract.

Nn

N is for **Navel**

Navel is one name,
and belly button is another,
for the place where you were once
connected to your mother.

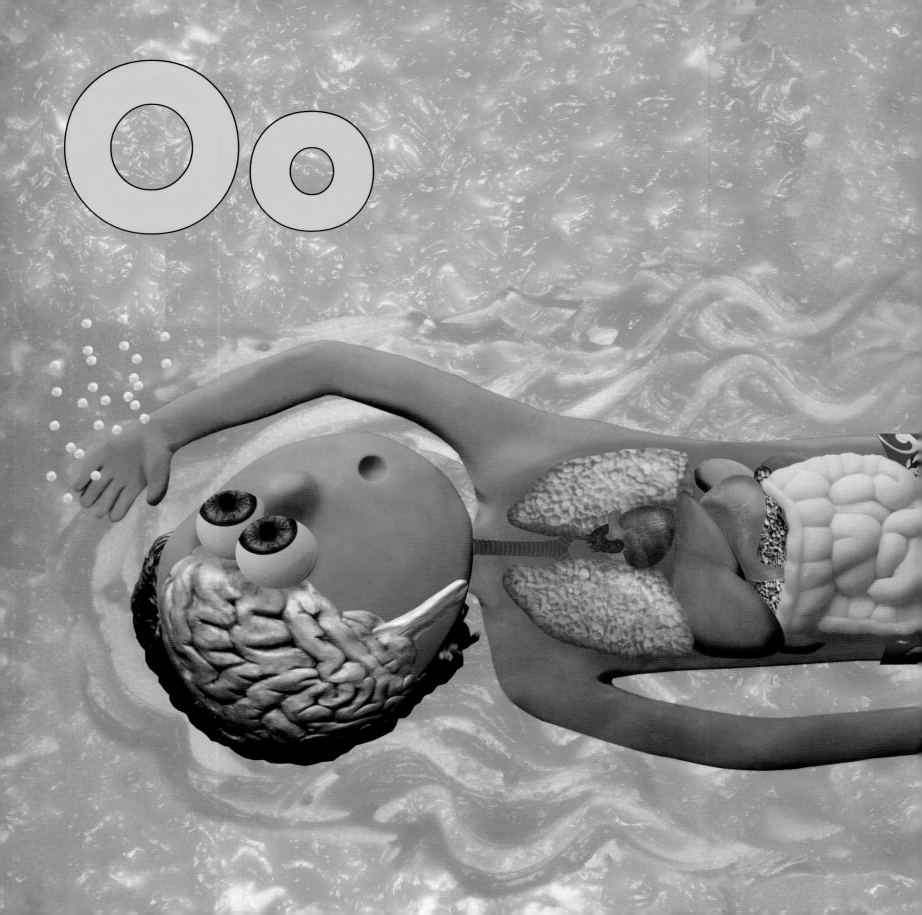

O is for Organs

Cleaning and pumping blood
are some jobs that organs do.
Your lungs and heart are organs,
and your skin's an organ, too!

P is for **Pupil**

The pupil is an opening
in your eye that lets in light.
It gets bigger when it's dim or dark
and smaller when it's bright.

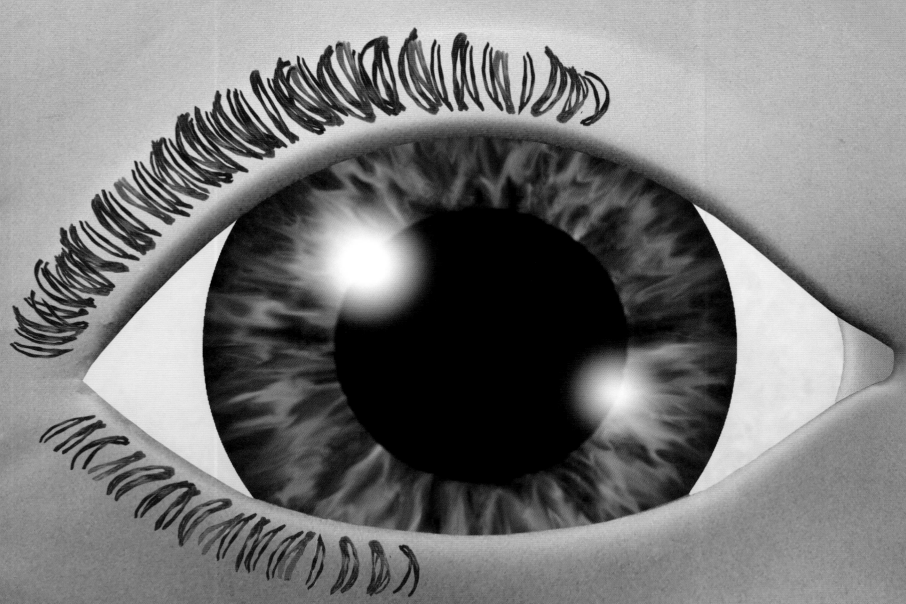

Q is for **Quadriceps**

This group of four strong muscles
lets you sit down on a chair.
It also helps you walk and run,
or jump up in the air!

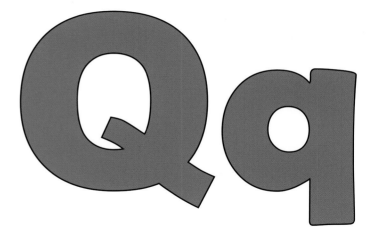

Rr

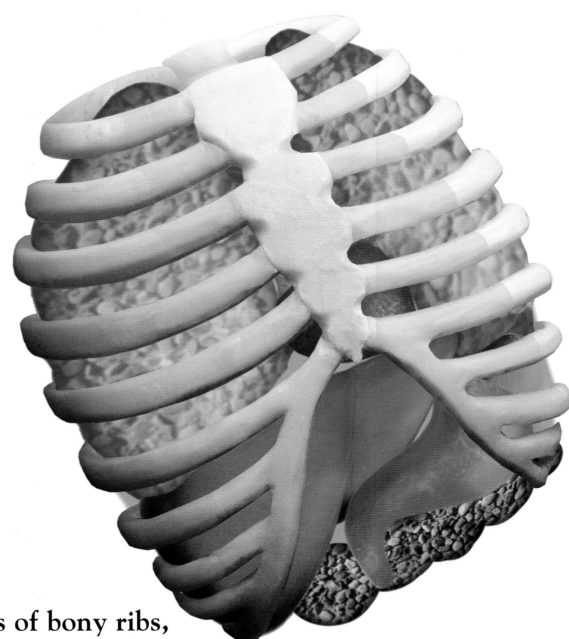

R is for Ribs

You have twelve sets of bony ribs,
and on your spine they connect.
The heart and vital organs
are what your ribs protect.

S is for **Skeleton**

If you looked through skin with X-ray eyes
a skeleton would be seen.
It's the structure of all the body's bones—
and a costume for Halloween!

Tt

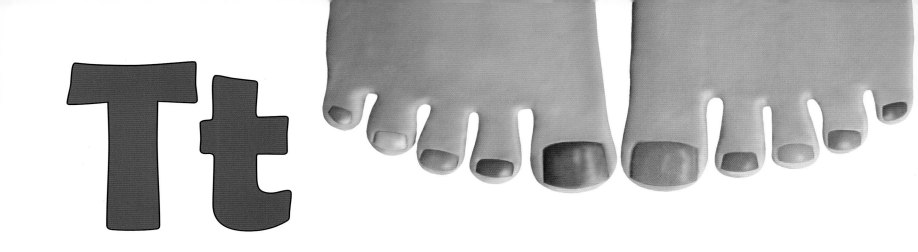

T is for **Toes**

When you walk from here to there
or join in sports with lots of action,
the ten toes on your feet
help give you balance and traction.

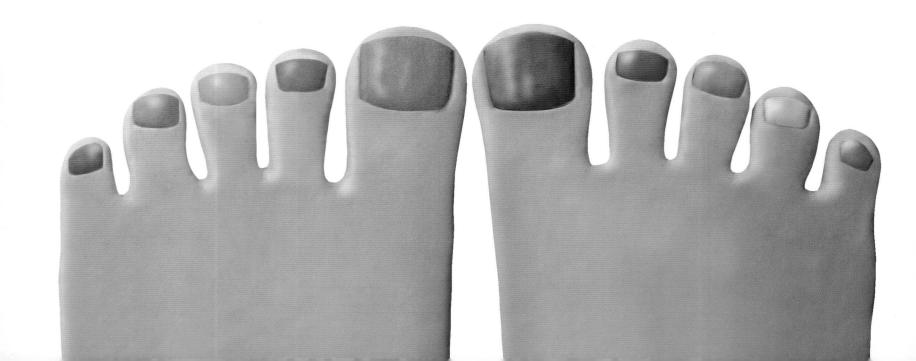

U is for Uvula

You might blame your uvula
if snoring is what you do.
It hangs down from your palette
and is shaped like the letter "U".

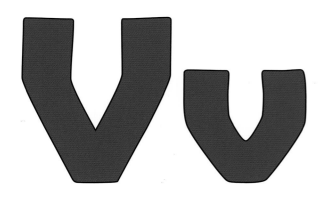

V is for Veins

Blood is pumping to your heart
every night and every day.
When it travels through your veins
it only flows one way.

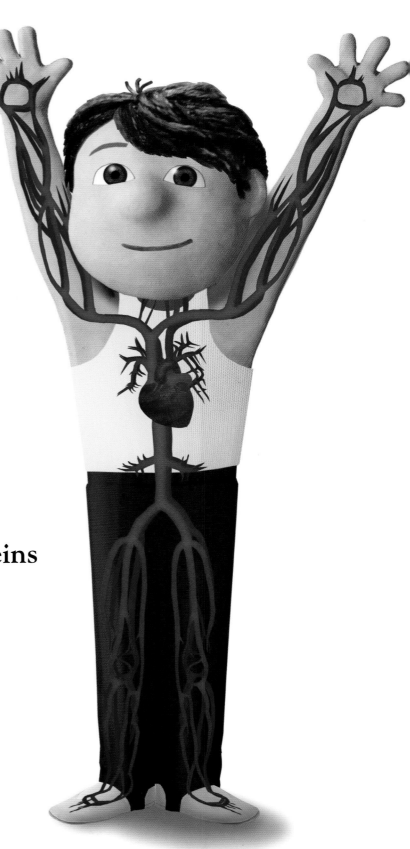

W is for **Wisdom Teeth**

You have a mouth that's full of teeth—
so show your pearly grin!
Your wisdom teeth will be the last
of your molars to grow in.

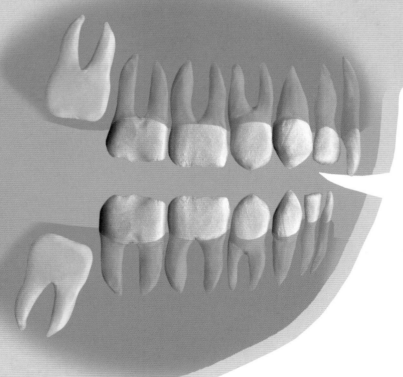

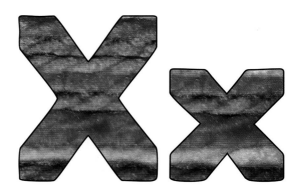

X is for X chromosome

Chromosomes store information about your gender, looks and more. Each girl has two X chromosomes of that you can be sure.

Y is for Y chromosome

Boys also have sex chromosomes—
one called Y and one called X.
There are 23 pairs of chromosomes.
They're tiny and complex.

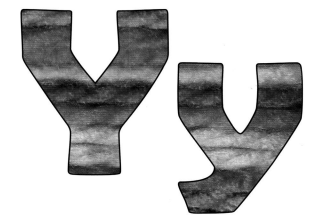

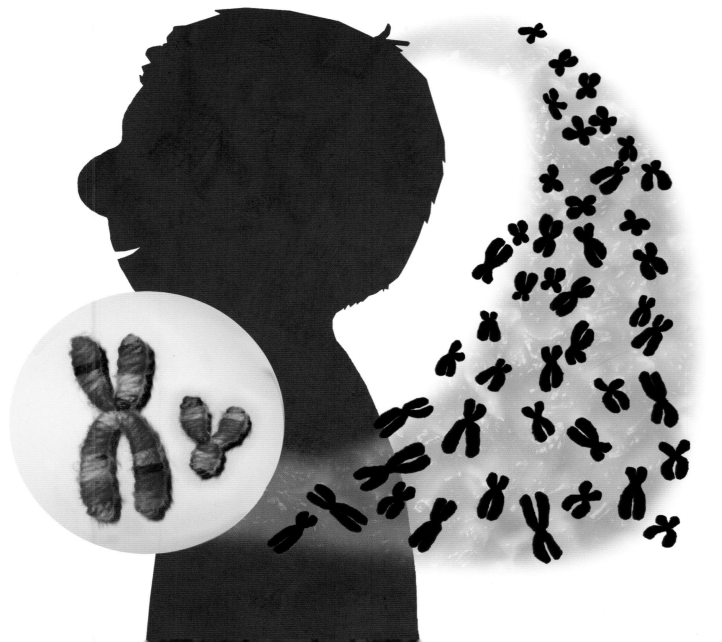

Z is for Zygote

You started your life as just one cell called a zygote, tiny and new. That cell then divided again and again and the end result was you!

Glossary

ANATOMY Anatomy is the study of the structures of the human body. Scientists research all the body parts, including bones, organs, blood, muscles and more, to learn how the body works. Doctors use this knowledge to treat illnesses and to help people stay healthy.

BRAIN The brain is like a command center for the body, controlling almost everything a person does. It is an organ that is broken down into five parts: the brain stem, cerebrum, cerebellum, hypothalamus and the pituitary gland. The cerebrum is the largest part, making up almost all of the brain's weight.

CELLS Trillions of cells make up the human body. There are more than 200 different kinds of cells. At the center of each cell is the nucleus, which contains all the information or the pattern that makes up a person.

DIGESTIVE SYSTEM The digestive system is made up of long, winding tubes and organs that break down and process food to turn it into the energy needed to nourish cells and provide fuel to muscles.

EARS Ears collect invisible sound waves and send them to the brain. The sound waves hit the eardrums, causing them to vibrate. The vibrations are interpreted by the brain as sounds. Ears not only allow a person to hear, but they have sensors that work together with the eyes, joints, muscles and feet to let the brain know the body's position.

FINGERPRINTS There are different patterns on fingerprints called loops, whorls and arches. Some people have a mixture of some or all of these patterns. Because no two people have the same fingerprint, police often use them to identify people.

GLUTEUS MAXIMUS *Gluteus maximus* is the scientific name for the muscle in the rear end. The *gluteus maximus* is the largest muscle in the human body. It is so large and strong because it is responsible for keeping the upper half of the body, also known as the trunk, upright. It is also used to make many movements, such as bending, sitting, running and jumping.

HEART The heart is a muscular organ that has a very important job— it pumps blood throughout the body. Blood gives the body necessary oxygen and nutrients. It is important to keep the heart strong and healthy by exercising and eating nutritious food.

IMMUNE SYSTEM The immune system is made up of cells, bone marrow and organs, such as the kidneys, spleen and skin. The complex network of cells and organs works to fight off germs that cause illness when they enter the body.

JOINTS There are two types of joints, hinged joints and fixed joints. The hinged joints allow bones to move, similar to how a hinge allows a door to move. Fixed joints don't move at all and are found in places like the skull.

KERATIN Keratin is a protein that is found in the upper layer of the skin, nails and hair.

LUNGS The two lungs are located in the chest. They are pink and spongy, and with the help of the diaphragm, they fill up with air that is breathed in and they empty as air is breathed out. There are two large airways leading to the lungs called bronchial tubes.

MUSCLES Muscles are fibers that tighten and relax to allow parts of the body to move. Some muscles can be moved voluntarily, like leg or arm muscles and others cannot be controlled by thought, like the heart muscle.

NAVEL Every person was once attached to his or her biological mother in the womb by an umbilical cord. When a person is born, the umbilical cord is cut and the spot where it was attached becomes the navel. Many people call the navel the belly button.

ORGANS Every organ in the body has a job to do. The heart's job is to pump blood and the kidneys' job is to clean blood. The skin is actually the largest organ in the body. The skin's function is to keep harmful bacteria, foreign substances and water from entering the body, as well as preventing fluids from leaving the body. Organ systems are two or more organs that work together. For example, the brain and spinal cord make up the central nervous system.

PUPIL The pupil is the central opening in the eye and it changes sizes depending on how much light there is in an environment. The colored area around the pupil is called the iris and it controls the size of the pupil.

QUADRICEPS The *quadriceps* is a group of four very strong leg muscles located in the top portion of the thigh. The muscles work together to allow the knees to extend.

RIBS Most humans have twelve sets of ribs, but sometimes a person is born with more or less. Together, the rib bones form the rib cage and protect vital organs such as the heart, lungs, spleen and kidneys. The rib cage also protects the backbone and breastbone.

SKELETON All the bones in the body form a structure called a skeleton. The skeleton holds up the body. Without it, there would be no support and people would not be able to stand, sit or walk. There are 206 bones in an adult body and over half of these bones are located in the hands and feet.

TOES The purpose of toes is to give people balance and traction when they are walking, running or standing on their feet. There are two bones in the big toe and three bones in the other four toes, for a total of fourteen small toe bones in each foot.

UVULA The uvula is the small u-shaped piece of tissue that hangs down from the soft palette in the back of your mouth. The uvula can contribute to snoring. The uvula and the soft palette together help food from entering the nasal cavity when you swallow.

VEINS There are miles and miles of veins in the human body. They are tiny tubes that carry blood back to the heart. Inside most veins are flaps that act like valves, to make sure that blood flows only in one direction. Veins work closely with arteries, which are the small tubes that carry blood away from the heart.

WISDOM TEETH Most adults have 32 teeth, sixteen on top and sixteen on bottom, including six pairs of molars, the big teeth in the back of the mouth used for chewing food. The last four molars to grow in are the wisdom teeth. Despite their name, they don't make you wiser!

X CHROMOSOME Chromosomes are strands of DNA wound tightly together that are inside every cell in the body. DNA holds instructions for the body to make all of its parts. There are 23 pairs of chromosomes in each cell. The 23rd set are the sex chromosomes and they determine a person's gender. Only females have two X chromosomes. Males have one X and one Y.

Y CHROMOSOME The Y chromosome carries approximately 250 genes and is responsible for male reproductive organs. If the 23rd set of chromosomes contains one Y chromosome and one X chromosome, the gender of that person is male. Only males have a Y chromosome.

ZYGOTE When two cells, one from a female and one from a male, merge together, they form a zygote, which will develop into an embryo about two weeks later. The embryo then grows into a human baby!

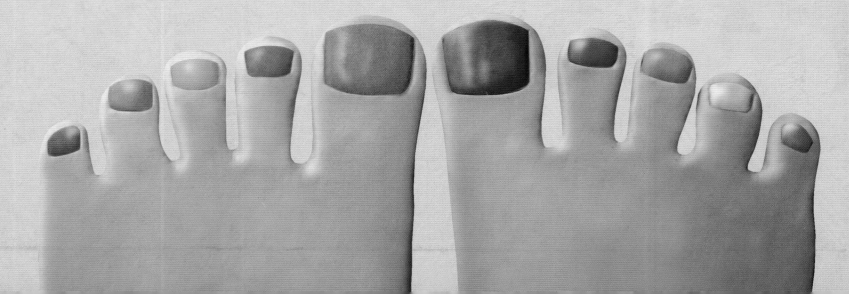

Body A to Z

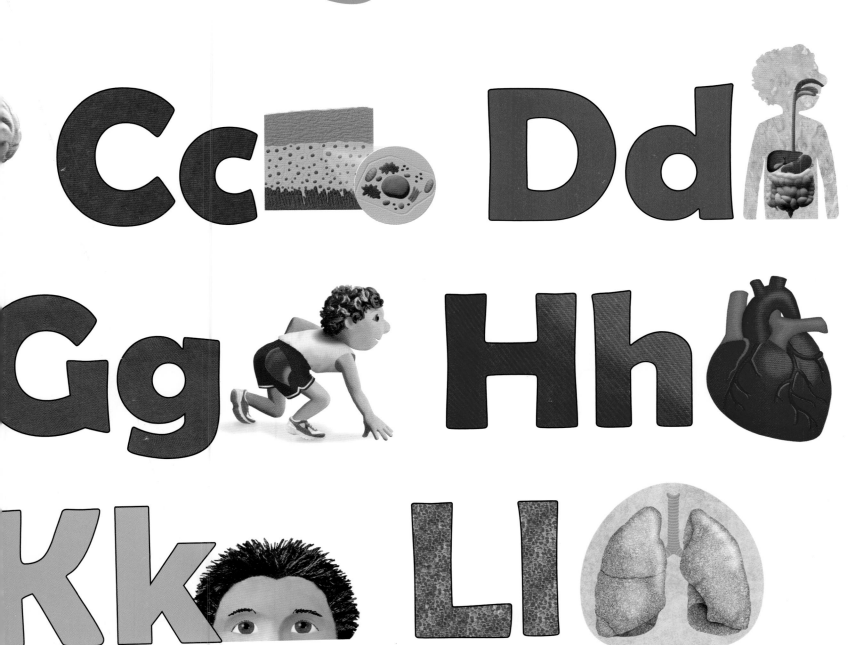

www.soundprints.com

Human

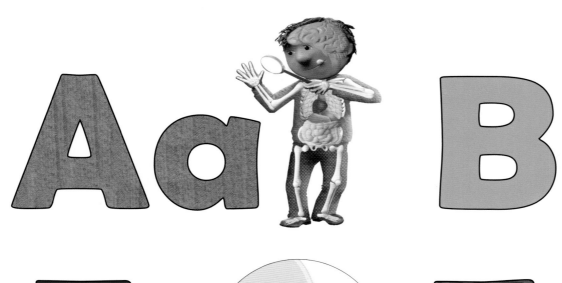

Aa Bb

Ee Ff

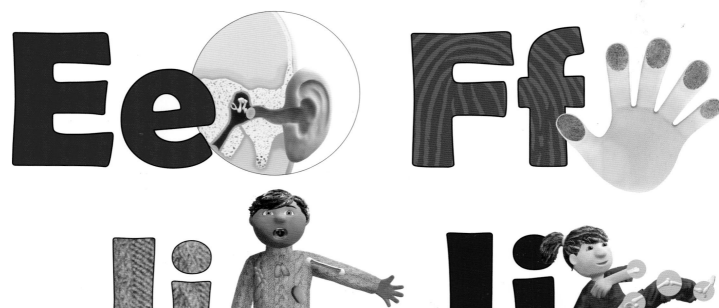

Ii Jj